PRAISE FOR OLIVER LEWIS

& *YOU'RE NOT THE ONLY ONE:*

"Exquisite! A book to treasure. I hope this has reached many young people along the way."
-online review

"Very touching, extremely heartfelt, beautifully written."
-reader review

"A rising star in the literary world."
"Oliver Lewis is reaching for the stars!"
-InYourArea

oliver lewis

OLIVER LEWIS

YOU'RE NOT THE ONLY ONE

& OTHER TALES OF SEVENTEEN

You're Not The Only One & Other Tales From Seventeen
 by Oliver Lewis
Infinity Publishing
 Copyright © UK Edition: August 20th 2022
Oliver Lewis - All rights reserved. No portion of this book may be reproduced in any form without permission from the publisher.

Cover design by Oliver Lewis.
Cover and back images: WatercolourWorld
Interior illustrations by: carlafcastagno, grandfailure, dannywilde & nataliia tossun

please be aware that this collection contains sensitive content that some readers may find upsetting/distressing relating to homophobia/homophobic slurs, bullying, anxiety and some sexual references.

contents:

13   you're not the only one

87   it breaks you up

166   off-centre theatrics

171   we lay, i fear

174   is this how it's going to be now?

175   ...on society

176   shoals

177   lost boy

180   why does this pen of mine always find anger?

181   post-gathering

182   it breaks you up: unseen letter

183   dear all cotton wool spinsters

184   miscellaneous entries of emmett dowry

188   warhol & a friend: artsy sex

190   eighth in drag

194   notebook pages

196   acknowledgements & afterword

199   about the author

201   me, us and the moon (memo)

To all those brave enough to create art. Even in these times, expressing yourself can be a great challenge.

YOU'RE NOT THE ONLY ONE

AUTHORS NOTE

You're Not The Only One is a book that changed my life. As dramatic as this sounds, it is the plain truth. I'd written a lot previous to this, but none of them projects allowed me to inject much of my own experience, feelings or world-view into them—nor did I have the confidence to do so at the time. Writing fiction, ironically, to me as a writer, means realism. I find that fiction is most powerful with a passion behind it, as with any artform, and from my reading perspective, I've found that the most passionate works tend to be those where the author (implicitly or explicitly) lays their heart out to the audience. This doesn't necessarily mean revealing detailed accounts of their private lives, but when their storytelling has more nuanced or heartfelt touches, or even whole plotlines that mean something to them, it gives the story they tell all kinds of magic and power.

I started writing this book, at the time titled *Blossom,* as a naïve little fifteen-year-old who had no idea who they were or why I felt certain feelings. The manuscript sat for a couple of years and was properly picked up again in 2020. After coming out, I managed to comprehend my feelings a little, and the main way I learned about myself and explored some of my questions was by writing this book. It was a confusing time, and things are still confusing now, but this story allowed me to gain clarity to a certain extent; for that, I owe it a lot.

By no means is this book a *deep* exploration of my own queerness, or queerness in general, but it was a starting point. A starting point for my writing of queer stories and finding myself in fiction.

I am glad that I have had the opportunity to revisit *You're Not The Only One,* and give it a breath of fresh air. By no means am I trying to re-write the past, as then it would be impossible to move forward, but in hindsight, two books down the line, I feel that I can enhance this story now I have developed my sense of self in the LGBTQ+ community, and in my general outlook on fiction. Hopefully this story can now be read as a more rounded one, and also read more in-line with my voice as a young, queer writer.

As I begin to type any new project, I feel a new spark of creative motivation, not just to tell a story, but to tell one that matters and means something to me—that may be a tiny aspect of a surreal plotline, or an entire character arc. Either way, this book is where I first felt that flame, and ever since publishing it, I've felt this burning desire to write more, observe what's happening around me, and look inwards to use writing as a way to converse with myself.

This book will always be a memorable chapter in my life, the start of something.

Oliver Lewis, July 2022.

PROLOGUE:
NERVES

If you're reading this,
I'm glad, but also,
I'm nervous.

And that's okay,
we're all nervous sometimes.

if you feel like, when you reach the end—
if you reach the end,
that this story was written for you,
it was.

If you live through this narrator
for the next few hours,
days,

weeks,

be honest with yourself,

if only for a mere moment.

If you are high on the possibilities of the dark,

just know that one day,

you will be high on the possibilities of the light too.

If all, or even some of these words

you seem to be a part of;

words of angst, joy, uncertainty, and pride,

I hope that you have a small epiphany…

You're not the only one.

CHAPTER ONE:
SUMMER

Sometimes I wonder why
I am not like them.

/

The birdsong this afternoon is beautiful
and loud,
even over the sound of traffic.

I'm leaving school pleased,
I got the grades I wanted,
and walk away without a glance back.

I'll probably never set foot in there again.

Starting sixth form next year,
same place as my friends.

Hopefully the people there won't be like those
where I've just left.

Not everyone was 'bad' of course,
but a minority can be a lot
when you feel alone.

I'm pacing frantically,
an excitement in my step.
I decide to take the long way home,
so that I don't come across the ones who call me
queer
as an insult.

Isn't it scary to know that
people can use your
truth
as an insult.

But they're not here,
so I can focus all my energy on being excited
for tonight.

In just a few hours, I'll be with my friends,
singing along to songs that mean everything to me.
Songs that have been with me through
the roughest of times,
and the happiest of times.

I simile,
I embrace the sunshine,

I breathe in the
sweet
Summer
air.

/

I read lots of books.

Many people talk about the importance of a
d i v e r s e
case,
and I dismissed it,
but it really is important.

Diversity is all around us
and we are all part of it,
the bubble of diversity,
in out own little ways.

/

When I arrive home,
I am greeted by the cheerful guitar riffs of my
'indie' playlist.

My three best friends:
Archie,
Elijah,

and George
are sitting in the living room.

I can faintly hear my Mum pottering in the kitchen,
but hardly.

Hiya Leo darling, I hear her shout.

Leo!
Elijah greets me, the other two smile.
Slouched on the sofa,
still in their college attire.

I grin and fall back onto the sofa between them,
dropping my bag onto the floor.

That's it, you're done, George says.
With school, with GCSEs, he means.
Nodding, I reply: Yeah, I guess so.

I can't help the corners of my lips curling up slightly
a faint smile surfacing.
I chuckle, shake my head a little
and say: I'm *done*!
Archie laughs at me.

/

I head up to my room
to get changed for the concert.
I don't know what to wear.

I stare at my wardrobe,
trying not to dwell on the matter,
but I can't help staring at my clothes,
notice how
mundane
they seem.

Muster up the confidence
and wear what you want, Leo.

Alas, I dress in black jeans and a mustard yellow sweater.
I stare out of the window for a moment,
and roll up my jeans a little.

Leo?
I hear George say, outside the door.
You ready?
Yeah, I reply.

And then:
one of the upmost difficult questions to answer.

So casually, like it's nothing,
and of course to normal people it *is* nothing.
But to me…

How
you
feeling
?

Despite the weight of the question,

we always tend to reply with something like:
I'm good
I'm fine.

Fine.
Fine?

What does
                    fine
even mean?

It hardly sounds like you're firing on
all cylinders,
does it?

Maybe sometimes it's worth being honest with ourselves,
for not today.

CHAPTER TWO:
MUSIC

We need to leave in an hour,
so whilst we wait,
drinks are opened and conversations are had.

I bet you're excited for A-Levels, eh?
Elijah nudges me,
and I smile because he's smiling,
and seeing my friends smile makes me smile.

Thank god I'm done with that
maths and science shit, I sigh.
Relief.

All I've ever wanted to do is create,
tell stories,

learn the art of telling storytelling.

And I know you think I'm mad,
and that's fine.

/

We walk to the train station from my house.

On the stroll, we discuss Italy,
reminding each other to be round mine early on
Monday morning,
not to forget passports.

Pack whatever we want,
because the only people seeing us,
is us,
not that that should make a difference,
but sadly,
it does.

/

Because it's a Summer night,
the sun is just beginning to set.

Up above is a beautiful ombre of orange,
with red streaks through the remaining clouds,
like veins of lava
seeping through the sky.

The train station is in sight now,

it's floodlights at the entrance piercing through the dusk,
and I feel a light sting of disappointment
that the lights are ruining Nature's dramatic display,
but pleased and giddy as they beckon me closer to the platform,
closer to the concert.

Closer.

/

Our carriage is

empty

and

quiet

/

A few weeks ago,
I read a book.

When I finish the book,
I'm crying.

It was about two boys,
meeting.

Finding their place
in the world.

It just caught me off guard,
spoke to me.

To *me?*

I've never felt this before.
                    Lost
but also like I've
                    found
something,
deep inside of me that was always there,
but waiting for the right moment
                                                            to
                                surface.

/

Another few weeks ago...

It was so hot that day,
yet the grass still a little damp.
It was early on, that's why,
a bit of dew still lingering on
the pointed tips of the grass.

The sun was up.

We sat on the ground, picnic blanket below us,
books scattered around.
There were classics
(battered spines an'all, yellowed pages, creased front covers)
There were new releases, some of our favourites,

some one of us liked, and the other didn't.

Elijah's speaker blasted out various songs.

After a dispute about song choices,
Archie and George pushing each other about,
us laughing.
They jump up and leg it across the field.
Tackling each other to the ground,
we laugh at them
because like they're two little kids.
As is everyone at heart,
I suppose.

/

There's something calming about
hustle and bustle,
which sounds strange.

And yes, this is a strange thought,
but there's something calming,
quiet,
comforting,
about blending it.

In a busy city centre,
you blend in like you're invisible,
eavesdropping on various people's conversations,
just snippets,
as they pass you by, barely acknowledging your existence.

You are in your own world,
in your own head,
with only those you care to be there with.

You may go about your business,
careless of the judgement of those around you.

As long as you can blend in,
you can be yourself
to an extent…

That being society's expectations of us.

The societal expectations that fester like maggots in flesh
with
privilege
of being *white*
of being *straight*
of gender, and identity
of anything outside of the
straight, white man.

So maybe, we'll never be able to fully
express ourselves,
be authentically ourselves,
unless this fucking society of ours bucks up it's ideas.

That's all to say,
we're in the city centre,
making our way to the venue.

/

The rumbling bass of the first support act
thrums through me as I stand at the bar:
I ask for a lemonade,
which Elijah will probably mix with vodka
from his hip flask.

Merchandise is pinned tediously to a board,
t-shirts stretched out to the point
where they could quite possibly tear.
The least appealing way
to display a shirt,
and yet I still want to buy one.

The concrete floor is sticky
with condensation and spilled alcohol,
shoes squeaking as we walk towards the standing entrance,
the bass becoming bolder,
and the doors swing open.

Our tickets are scanned,
and the music envelops us.

/

Its quite difficult to explain the
feeling you get at a concert.

…surreal

Alas, the support acts had been and gone,
and the venue filled to the brim with people.

Loud, muffled chatter surrounds us.

You ready?
Archie asks, shouting so I can hear him.
I'm ready Archie, I'm so fucking ready.
He, in reply, smiles and throws his arm around me.

Almost as if on cue,
the lights dim and darkness wraps itself around us.

Blue lights create a faint, dim glow from behind the stage,
allowing us to see the blurred silhouettes of the band
as they make an entrance,
being ever closer to filling the venue
with the most
beautiful noise.

/

The sound of
You're Not The Only One
fills the hall,
and I could cry.
I do cry.

When I blink,
I keep my eyes shut for just a second longer than usual,
taking a moment to be in my own head,
but also not wanting to miss anything happening around me.

George knows what this song means to me,
so he subtly looks,

a small but sure smile spreads across his face.
I look back for a small, mere second,
and he looks at me like there's something *worth* looking at.

There's a light in his eyes,
and I am to him,
as he is to me,
briefly gorgeous.

A sensitive moment,
where the music is too loud,
and yet,
it is not loud enough.

/

Being at an airport at
4AM is
serene.

It is quiet, the occasional clack of footsteps
echoing in the foyer.

Your eyes hardly open.

Happy to be here, yet simply don't want to be here.

How strange.

How serene.

/

We're on the cheapest flight to Italy
we could possibly find,
but it's surprisingly exhilarating.
For such a small cost,
you are about to travel such great distance.

Is this true in life occasionally?

Three of us are squashed together on a row,
and Elijah sits across the aisle from us looking slightly
creeped out by wrinkly old white guy next to him.

The man's gilet (seemingly as old as him) brushes
Elijah's shoulder
and he looks across at us with a face of
(comedic) disgust.

The plane hums loudly,
as if it were a living, breathing being.

But it is simply a machine.
Simply a machine.

/

Upon the plane's landing
there was a cheer.

A wall of heat hits us as we exit the plane,
into the Italy heat.

The air is dry, but it is sweet.

It is sweet with the taste of
freedom,
and of weeks of
reading,
exploring,
getting lost in music,
of sunsets,
of laughter.

The air is dry,
but it is sweet.

The sickly sweet taste of freedom.

CHAPTER THREE:
ITALY

The hotel was cheap,
but it's good enough for us.

Elijah throws his suitcase at the foot of the bed,
before collapsing backwards onto it.

I pull of a battered paperback of
The Invisible Life of Addie LaRue.

You can read your favourite book over and over,
it'll never get old.

And after the noise of travelling,
and airports
and buses,

it is, for now,
quiet.

/

Dawn breaks, new beginnings.

The Italy sun is welcoming us.
An incentive to venture into the maze of cobbles.

I crack open the window next to my bed,
looking out over the (usually busy) street below,
but there is not a soul
                in sight,
                an insight
into the town,
before the early risers
        amble the alleyways.

The Sun,
at work before anyone else.
        Warming the waters:
        lakes, ponds, brooks, the sea
                                cerulean as it is.

The plans receive the affection they need.

Light and life.

/

Elijah is surfacing from sleep now,

so I get some coffee on.

The kettle in the room is small,
and it lets out a low hiss, a hum, whirring to life.

It is loud, like everything.
Everything seems louder in the morning.

/

I check my Instagram feed and find nothing new.

The latest photo is one from my old school,
it's of the football team.

Being simply curious, I take a look at the rest of the profile.

There's the boys football team again,
and the boys rugby team,
and the boys basketball team,
and...

What about the netball team,
and that one boy in year ten
who stuck up the middle finger to every other
boy in his year that shouted:
you big fucking girls blouse!

That was two years back,
and I remember seeing this kid strut out
of the training session with a huge grin on his face.

And I remember sitting
and talking to him that lunch.

And I remember being envious
of his confidence

He probably got the same shit as me,
the 'gay' as an insult malarkey,
and getting pushed off your bike on the way to school.

Here is the school's social media,
full of pictures of those very boys.

Maybe the school are oblivious.
Or maybe they just turn a blind eye.
That'll do the trick.

/

We met George and Archie in the hotel lobby,
ready to head out on our first day.

Good sleep?
I ask as way of greeting.
Well, Archie begins, as good as it could have been
with a bed made of chipboard.
Stop complaining!
George shoved Archie's shoulder.
It's just *honesty* George, he laughs.
Alas, I lighten the mood, breakfast calls!

/

Upon exiting the hotel
and beginning out stroll along the sun-streaked streets,
it is quiet as we take in the architecture around us.

There are wooden crates that line people's balconies
filled to the brim with flowers of great vibrancy,
like an overflowing box of fruits,
ripe and delightful.

There are pools of morning sunlight
where it spills through the gaps in the narrow,
dainty lanes.

The front porches and doorsteps of the terraced houses
seem to all have their very own personality,
fastidious in their appearance.
        Each terracotta pot is delicately and thoughtfully placed,
        as the plants bask and rejoice
        in the warmth of Summer.

/

The café we stop at for breakfast
is tucked away in a streetside nook,
as are many places around here.

It seems we're surrounded by a fair few
early risers too,
and it is understandable that many may want
to get breakfast outside before the hear of midday gets
too searing.

Woah, Elijah mumbles as the food arrives,
looking up at the three of us like it's Christmas morning,
and he's five years old.

And to be fair, his expression is justified.

My pancakes are stacked hight,
dusted with icing sugar and topped with strawberries.
Maple syrup slowly drips from the top pancake,
down the stack,
and into the golden pool on the plate below.,

Elijah's steaming pastries have a beautiful aroma,
butter melts into the cracks of the bread rolls,
and small pots of jam and marmalade sit on the side.

Archie and George's apple cake
has sugar on top of it,
making the tiny crystals glisten in the sunlight.

The espresso is dark,
bittersweet, tangy and soothing
all at once.

/

~before~

Would you like to introduce yourself?
asks a woman on the opposite me in the circle.

She has large hoop earrings,

and is wearing a polka dot jumpsuit.
She leads this discussion group,
and to be honest, as lovely as she is,
I'm scared and I'm nervous.

I'm Leo. I'm sixteen.
Everyone is looking at me, but it's not in an intimidating way,
in a caring and supportive way.
And I'm gay. I think, no—yeah, I'm gay. That's all.
I paused for a few seconds, gathering my unhealthily dishevelled
thoughts.
I mean. I'm still—I'm still figuring stuff out, you know?

S
T
U
T
T
E
R

T
R
A
I
L
I
N
G

Yeah...

O F F

S
  T
   U
     T
   T
     E
  R

Thank you for that Leo, Says the nice lady
It's wonderful to have you here.

Also in the circle there's:

An older man who has been stripped of his confidence after
being victim to a homophobic hate crime at his workplace.

Someone who is coming to terms with their gender identity.

A boy called Archie,
similar age to me,
has brown skin, fingers adorned with silver rings,
looks unbelievably nervous, but I'm pretty sure this isn't his first
time,
like me.
I'm Archie, and being bisexual and a person of colour
in my school gets me into trouble with
some of the people in my year
and they
chat a load of shit
about me
and I just
don't

understand
why
and I need
to
talk
about it
please.
I hope
that's okay.
I'm rambling,
sorry.

The other boy next to him
(Elijah. I've just transitioned, and I feel
more *myself than*
ever.
But, sometimes I still feel
unsure
and
scared
around people.)
Puts his hand on Archie's thigh
as if to say
it's alright.

And then there's
(George, and I'm not sure where I fit in,
and that's a little intimidating. I mean—I'm not straight,
I know that, but
I don't really—I need to figure things out.)

In this moment, I knew I'd met some
beautiful people.

CHAPTER FOUR:
NOTES FROM A
DISCUSSION GROUP

Labels.
Sometimes confusing.
Often used
to define
you.

/

If
the world
wasn't full
of bigots,
we wouldn't need
labels.

/

Each to
their own.

For some,
they help.

For some,
they don't.

But they always
give a name
to marginalised
groups.

So their
voice
can be
heard
over the
hate.

/

Hate
is a
strong
word,
shame we
have to use
it to

describe
some people's
attitudes
and
actions
against
us.

/

Understand and embrace our
diversity.

Otherwise
progress
will
freeze

/

If you are
silent
about past trauma
or a
bad
experience,
it will grow like a
weed
in the deepest pit of your stomach
and blister.

An ulcer.

/

Although the world around
may inflict rage within us,
there's always someone
who can help
snuff the flames.

CHAPTER FIVE:
DISCOVERY

Do I look good?
George asks.

We're in some thrift shop,
and he's found these
huge heart-shaped sunglasses.

Simply stunning, I say bluntly.
Smiling.

The old lady who owns the store
is glancing up from her crossword giving us
disapproving looks.

And we laugh.

/

The rest of the day continues similarly.

We stop for lunch
before exploring the streets further.

The architecture is still striking
and exquisite.

Archways curving eloquently,
inviting folk into whatever is on the other side.

Intricate floral and historical carvings
detail the stone and plaques that lean against the pillars.

To think,
these passages have been here
long before me,
and long before anyone around.

So rather than being overwhelmed by the
cacophony of traffic and other commotion,
we are enveloped by bubbly and cheerful chatter.

We are blanketed by the scent of
bakeries, coffee, and musky perfume.

/

It is remarkable, really.

I've never felt so...

peaceful.

This is truly,
infinitely,
wonderful.

/

Days go by,
and I lose track of time.

Lost in the entrancingly
never-ending nights.

Lost in the beauty of this place,
and the people who surround me.

/

A bumblebee buzzes
under my nose.

Rather than flinch,
or pull away from it,
I watch it closely.

The way it simply hovers there
for a few seconds,
before whizzing off to find
a delectable flower.

Allow Nature to breathe,
you'll get along
just fine.

/

on that thought

There are no rules
in this life of ours.

We are small
in the grand scheme of things.
But the most minute moments,
emit love.

/

Nearing the end of our second week in Italy,
we find a field
in the middle of nowhere,
and watch the
s
  u
    n
      s
        e
          t

/

When it's almost

                    pitch black,
we all switch on our phone torches so we can
see each other still.

Amongst general conversation,
Archie, who's been deep in thought asks:
Why do we have to come out?
What'd you mean?" Asks Elijah.
Like, *why*? Who says we *have* to come out?

We all sit there puzzled.
Because all four of us have already come out,
it's not something that's really
crossed out minds.

I dunno.
is all I can say.

Well, Elijah begins
I don't see why it's a thing either.
I mean, *straight* people don't have to come out,
so I suppose it's just a societal expectation.
The 'norms' in society are clear, because if being who *you are*
doesn't affect you negatively in any way, you fit into societal
normality,
but us queer kids,
we have to justify *our*
existence
to everyone.
Society has created it's very own mould,
and if you don't fit into it,
you need to let everyone know.

It's so *fucking* sad.

Who even came *up* with that?

It's not like we've never existed!
We've *always* existed.

That's the thing! I say.

And Elijah is right.

One day, hopefully,
we'll all be able to fit in seamlessly.

/

Long into the night
we sing our favourite songs,
and drink cheap beer,
a laugh.

I look up at the sky,
and the stars gaze back at me.
They glisten,
like thousands of diamonds shattered across the
deep, never-ending blackness of the sky.

The moon stays hidden behind the odd cloud,
occasionally peeking out.

I guess we're all like a moon,
only showing certain aspects of ourselves.

A little at a time,
and when we're with the people we love most
on the clearest of nights,
we are completely ourselves.

Before the cycle starts all over again.

/

We all put in thirty Euro,
to buy a cheap record player at a vintage store.

The store is filled, stacked floor to ceiling
with a random assortment of items.

It's a good forty-minute walk back to the hotel,
and we toss a coin in a fountain.

The reflection of the small statue at it's centre
ripples and warps in the water below.

Hey!
George says, waving to himself in the
liquid mirror.

I soak up the history of my surroundings
as we walk.

/

Back at the hotel, we all go to George and Archie's room.

The new record player is plugged in.

As *Nica Libres At Dusk* plays out,
with it's delicate, floating guitar
sweeping across the room,
we sit and talk.

We talk about September,
about how relieved I am to be away from
some certain people from my now old school.

I realise why I love these friends so dearly.
It's because, with them,
I am simply me,
and they are simply them.

And in this emotional state of
saying why we love each other so much in a drunken daze,
and how proud we are about how far we've all come,
the hours fly by.

Once again, the night is upon us,
but the music plays on.

/

When I wake,
Elijah is reading a battered copy of *The Starless Sea*,
and I ask him:
How many times have you read that?

He chuckles quietly, the other two still flat-out.

Too many times, and yet, I always discover something new.

'There is a pirate in the basement...'
I whisper the opening lines of the book to myself,
which makes Elijah smile.

A pressing of *Hypersonic Missiles* it still sitting
dormant on the turntable.

Ever so quietly,
I go over and place the needle on the opening track.

It plays softly in the background,
and causes Archie and George to stir.

I take that as my sign with pour a cup of coffee.

/

I'm sad that it's our last full day in Italy.

/

We spent that evening at a lake.

You couldn't see the water's edge in the darkness,
so, we all walked slowly forward
until we felt the refreshing chill of the cool water at our ankles.

We counted down in unison,
before legging it into the lake.

Water splashed everywhere,
it stung my eyes.

We all found each other once neck deep,
and just like most nights here in Italy,
laughed and talked,
and sang dreadfully.

As ever, the stars were watching over us,
and they twinkled in delight at our joy.

I lay back and let myself float,
and it felt, in that moment,
like I was flying.

CHAPTER SIX:
FOREST

Figuring things out
for yourself
is difficult,
I know.

/

Imagine trekking
through a
forest.

Where the ground
is smooth
and nature
is kind.

/

You can stay
within
this forest
for as long
as you need.

/

The smooth ground
stops you
from
tripping

and everything
is on
your side.

/

The
nice
forest.

/

You build
your dream
home.

Everything you

ever wanted.

You feel
safer
than ever.

/

Someone stumbles
to the edge
of your
forest.

You are unsure
whether to let them
in or not.

If you do
they'll know
everything.

They will see your life,
your land,
your home.

They could set traps,
you could trip,
and fall.

They probably won't,
but
they

could.

/

"As long as you don't disturb anything."
You say.
"Simply love me and this forest just how it is."
You say.

CHAPTER SEVEN:
PRIDE

After arriving home,
I can't help but miss Italy.

But there's a knock on the door
that I've been waiting for since the minute
I woke up.

I swing the door open,
and Elijah stands on the doorstep looking
incredibly vibrant.

Wow!
I say.
Colourful, dude, matter-of-factly.
No shit, Elijah chuckles, Any chance I can come in?

God, yeah—sorry.

I have to admit,
It's so brilliant seeing him again.
Even though it's only been
a matter of days.

Soon after,
George and Archie arrive.

We all have our own huge flags,
and are dressed in bright colours.

It brings me so much joy.

Shall we head out, then?
George says.

/

As soon as we hit the city centre,
we see masses of people
that merge into one
huge rainbow.

Our eyes light up.

Streamers hang from balconies,
and people unapologetically blast out
Pet Shop Boys.

The music thrums through my whole being,

I shiver.
The hairs on the back of my neck stand on end.

There is loud chatter,
people joyfully yelling through megaphones,
whistles being blown,
and *even* a French Bulldog wearing a cloak.

I can't hear myself think
in the best way possible.
Thinking about nothing aside from this moment,
as we venture deeper into the celebration.

A parade float edges closer to us,
and people throw confetti from above.

I smile so fucking much.

The most beautiful and fascinating thing about this is,
every person I see here
has their own story.

I have mine,
George has his,
Elijah has his,
and Archie has his.

As does the person ahead of me,
as do all the people who brush past me.

Every time I meet the eyes of someone here,
I feel a warmth wrap around me,

care,
empathy,
love.

It's magic, and only magic.

/

I turn my back for one second,
and just like that,
Elijah is gone.

Where's he ran off to?
I ask the other two.
Where *has* he gone?
Archie startles.

We begin working our way
through the crowds,
looking for Elijah.

And as we turn our heads,
we see he's made his way onto a
huge parade float.

George literally cannot stop smiling.
LEO! LOOK!
Elijah yells,
flailing his arms all over the place.

He's tangled is a load of
streamers and now wearing a

sparkly hat someone must have given him.

GUYS, COME ON!
He beckons us over,
and we find our way to some steps
at the back of the float.

Elijah comes pacing over.
This is so *COOL!*
He shouts into my ear.
Pushing us further into the crowd.

This is the happiest I've ever seen him,
beaming smile, gesturing at everything.
Welcome aboard!
someone says from behind us.

So now we're actually a *part* of the parade,
seems we're on a float an'all.

A 2010's *Katy Perry* song blares from an amplifier,
and people wave and scream as we pass.

The four of us clap and sing along to the music,
it's a surreal moment.

I dance.
And I *never* dance—ever.

But here we are.
I don't know what I look like,
nor do I care to know.

Then we've all got arms round each other,
and we're jumping up and down
and we're yelling the lyrics to pop songs.

/

I've felt quite alone
before now,
It's easier than you think to become isolated
through your own thoughts.

/

All there needs to be is
belief.

Belief
that you can be
completely yourself.

In a world without repercussion.
One day.

/

In this splendid moment,
time is elastic.

/

Can I stay here forever?

/

Having a good time?
Archie asks me.
We've stepped out of the parade, just for a breather,
and food.
I give him a look.
Stupid question, I know, he laughs.
Of course I am.

I feel like—Archie pauses,
I feel like I understand myself a lot more,
you know?

I nudge him, smiling.
Yeah, I say, thoughtfully.

After a few seconds, I say:
I still question myself a bit.

Archie turns to face me.
That's alright, he says, warm toned.
How do you mean?

Well, I always said I was, like, gay.
But the—you know, *nitty-gritty*
has always been a burden. I don't...
I'm not sure I want *that.*
I've been sitting,
convincing myself I'm fucking weird.

I feel suddenly anxious,

and exposed.

But Archie just sighs, lightly, sympathetically.
I get you, he says.

I feel a wave of relief wash over me.

So you don't think that's *weird?*
I ask him.

He chuckles.
Of course I don't think you're weird, mate.
Everyone's different, people feel different things,
like and dislike all sorts of stuff.

Stuff?
I ask.

Archie smiles at me again.
You know what I mean,
feelings an' shit.
Anyway, being asexual is a thing!
Being attracted to people,
just romantically, rather than sexually.

The relief I felt—and still feel
starts to swell around me.

There's a whole spectrum,
but my point is, it's nothing out of the ordinary.

Thank you, I say.

Don't be ridiculous,
that's what were all here for, right?

Right, I smile.

The other two are there with us the whole time,
snacking on a cone of chips.

I turn the concept over in my mind,
and I think I will for a while.

/

We head back into the parade for
a final time.

Even as it starts going dark,
the streets are alive with colour and light.

As we walk by,
a confetti cannon blasts glitter
into the air.

The sky shimmers,
as it rains down on us
like glimmers of hope.

IT BREAKS YOU UP

Though you may not be able to sense the melancholic tone of my voice in writing, it is there, I promise. Because everyday I see you pass by. And you and you *and* you!

Their walk has a bounce, hair lightly flailing in the breeze. When I listen to some songs, they are in my head, but ever so far away. I could change, I *have* changed in the past, only briefly I'll add, but no matter what, the opportunity to act ebbs and flows, it fades away right before my eyes. It's like a sort of yearning, but that's a little dramatic, it's not that severe, really, more like an everlasting want, subtly, in the pit of my stomach. So many times you've said "cheers, mate" when I held open the door, at concerts, there with your friends…I swear you had your arm round that boy's shoulders the whole way through. You are everywhere I go, it seems. Ah, them short conversations, so rare, I prolonged as much as I could, but somehow my inner self told me to stop, show no interest. Strange, that. I've cursed myself so many times for letting go so easy. In one instance, you're gone. Something seems missing now, though we never really spoke. And every time, I've wanted to shout your name (if I knew it) and tell you, really, truly,

"I am here."

\-   *From Ethan Walker's Diary.*

PART ONE
FIGHT ON

Dear Ben,

Alright first day at college that, wasn't it? I mean, there's still loads of people I still need to meet, but it was nice to have you around. As in, we both have similar classes, interests et cetera. I also recall, during our conversation surrounding literature (we're both very interested in that kind of thing, it seems) we decided to maybe write each other a few letters. You've probably forgotten already, which is fair enough, but I thought I'd do one anyway. I think the whole idea stemmed from you going on about Emily Dickinson, and how her letters can reveal so much about her personality. I've ordered that edition, by the way. We've got very different tastes, but I think we may learn a lot from one another, supposing we remain friends. I wouldn't blame you if you thought I was a complete weirdo, and you just want to ignore me for the next two years of college. I'd get that.
 Alas, I suppose this is my first entry into our letter-writing-endeavor, of which you may not want to partake. I'll see you most days anyway. Hopefully.

Ethan x

Ps. I put a kiss at the end of everything, it's a habit. Sorry.

Ethan.

I am very much ready to embark on this 'letter writing endeavor', as you are calling it.

I found your letter tucked into the front pocket of my bag last night. Very subtle of you! The ink was kind of smudged, are you left-handed by any chance?

Amongst our extended discussion about Emily Dickinson, I mentioned that you should read The Pickwick Papers, and I'd like to remind you in case you didn't remember. It's one of Dickens' earliest works, it's pretty hilarious honestly, lots of slapstick kind of comedy. I really can't believe you've never read Dickens before, but this is a good place to start, I must say.

Also, I've been thinking about the fact you said you were struggling with one of the essay questions for English Literature, and I though maybe we could meet after school tomorrow and go through it together? It's up to you, don't feel obliged. Seriously.

As for that kid, was Aiden his name? who blurted that slur at you before, just ignore him. I know that it upset you, but he's just doing it for attention. I mean, did you see the reaction he got from the group of lads behind him? Exactly! If all else fails, you could just tell them to 'fuck right of'.

B.

Dear Ben,

I find your attitude towards homophobic dickheads quite admirable. Your simple solution of ignoring them or telling them to do one (in more explicit terms). I wish I could be like that, but I find it really difficult. Maybe you could teach me your ways. And yes, to answer your question, I am indeed left-handed. How do you notice such minute details of one's inky scrawl?

Thank you for helping me with the essay, by the way.

I was really anxious about meeting up with you outside of school, but it wasn't awkward at all, thankfully. I guess that shows we may have a good bond developing. Your house is really nice, also. It's convenient that it's only like a fifteen minute walk from mine. I like how—and I mean this in a good way, how 'higgledy-piggledy' it is. You described it as 'a mess', and 'stuff everywhere', but I love how much character your house has. The warm white lightbulbs, the kitchen with pots and utensils hanging on the wall, the living room with the crackling fire and the sofa that your dog, Bruce, seems to own. I haven't seen your bedroom yet, or any of the upstairs for that matter, as you *insisted* it needs to be tidied. Cheers for inviting me in. Despite it being 'essay-writing', it was a really enjoyable evening. You're a good person, you know that, right?

Ethan x

Ethan.

Thank you for your detailed description of my own house, I think I know it a little better now.
I'm glad you can see character in it, unlike me, maybe because I am used to it by now. I think that, once we get used to things, we kind of just forget about them, what they're worth, where we'd be without them. Should probably not take things for granted so much.

I had a really nice evening too. I'm actually sitting next to Bruce on the sofa now. My parents are out again tonight, so I'm not hibernating in my room upstairs. I haven't lit the fire though, I don't want to set the house alight. Maybe you should come round again at some point when I'm home alone, and we can light the fire, that way it'll be shared responsibility if the house burns down. It won't though, fingers crossed.

B.

TWO WEEKS LATER

Dear Ben,

Today was pretty chilled, right? Hardly any lessons, either of us, so we just sat right at the bottom of the field, round the corner a little where nobody could see us, and talked and talked. Maybe that could be our little spot now, away from all the madness inside. The conversation was so long I can barley remember the topics we covered! Something about French Bulldogs, you trying to convince me to go to a Pride parade, a new author obsession of yours…and we listened to Ben Howard's album *Collections From The Whiteout* which I found to be particularly beautiful, it's one of my favorites. That, amongst the sounds of the light breeze ruffling grass and birds singing.

I found our discussion about anxiety quite poignant. Without being too sentimental, I've began to feel an immense sense of trust between you and me, especially today. You really opened up, as did I, and I can't stop thinking about it, honestly. It's nice to know that we've had shared experiences. Talking about it helped a lot, maybe we should talk to each other about that kind of stuff more often. Thank you for trusting me enough to talk about the bullying you experienced in your old school, mostly because of your sexuality. Although I didn't mention it that much today, I was bullied too, for the same reason. I guess being gay in a UK secondary school isn't so easy still. Despite it being nowhere near as bad as my old school, I've still overheard some shit here that felt a little like an arrow to the chest. Have you ever felt like the room is closing in on you because of a conversation going on or a joke being made? Yeah, I've had that a few times now. I don't know about you?

Thinking about it, this is the first time in a very long time that I haven't spent a while mulling over the most tiny fragments of an interaction with someone. I told you about that, too, remember? How simply over the way I end a conversation with someone, I can think about it for a good while afterwards, always finding something to regret or that I shouldn't of said. The barley noticeable change of tone in someone's voice that makes me think I've said something wrong, slipped up somehow. It's not normal, I know. I'm glad you still want to be my friend even after me telling you all this about myself, that makes me seem like a nutter! I haven't really told anyone about it before. It can make me feel pretty shit sometimes. Thanks for listening to me and not running a mile. I appreciate it, seriously, I do.

Ethan x

Dear Ben,

Yes, I did walk to your house and post this letter without knocking to see if you'd want to talk in person, simply because I wasn't sure if you would be asleep or something. I'm assuming you weren't in school today because you have fallen ill. I hope you okay. If you are off for too long, I may feel like I need to go ahead with the all important *knock* and check up on you.

Other people are strangely daunting when you're not around. I don't really know what to do with myself. I feel disoriented, even though I am well-aware of where I am and what I'm doing. So weird.

Also, I really hope that my previous letter didn't scare you off. It got pretty deep.

Sorry.

Ethan x

The weekend came round soon enough. The Wednesday, Thursday and Friday Ethan had spent at college had flew by, despite the fact he didn't know what to do with himself. Ben was coming over to his today. He felt much better now. Ethan had indeed dropped off a hot flask of soup on

Thursday night at Ben's house.

It was a cold morning when Ben arrived, and upon his knock, Ethan padded down the stairs to the front door. Sure enough, there was Ben standing on the doorstep, a tote bag over his shoulder, dressed in stone-

coloured joggers, a white hoodie under a thick winter jacket.

Hey, Ethan said when he swung open the door.
Hey, Ben laughed a little.

Come in, come in! It's cold outside.

He said thanks as he slipped off his trainers.

Can I get you a drink at all? Coffee? I know you're a coffee fiend.

Following Ethan into the kitchen, he said: That'd be lovely, thanks.

After the coffee had been brewed and poured, the two of them sat at the

breakfast bar in the kitchen.

I hope my letter wasn't too deep, Ethan said.
Ben furrowed his brow a little. What do you mean?

Just didn't want to vent at you too much.

There was a pause for a few seconds, but it seemed like an eternity to Ethan, he just didn't know how to break the silence. Definitely not small talk. That's not natural conversation. Him and Ben always have natural conversation. So rather than shy away from the silent moments, he wallowed in them. And in this company, he felt strangely comfortable amongst the quiet. He anticipated the chatter beyond it would be worth the wait.

Ben looked down at his coffee, the light bubbles still vaguely swirling around on the surface, and said—almost whispered: It made me cry, you know.

What's wrong?

Nothing. I'm just saying, your letter, it made me cry.

Why did you say that so quietly? Are you ashamed of crying?

A little, yes.

It's alright, you know. I cry over a lot of things.

So do I.

There was another silence before Ben continued. You're not weird, he said. About all the overthinking stuff, I mean. We all see things in different ways. Evaluate our interactions in different ways. He trailed off.

Ethan sighs. It's not like that.

Look, Ben said, I know that I'll never be able to understand fully because I'm not you, but it might be some kind of anxiety. You can speak to people about it. Like, professionals.

Why can't I just speak to you?

You can. I'm just saying.

~

I'd assume you're feeling much better now? Ethan asked.

Yeah, thanks. The soup was much appreciated by the way. Soothed my throat, nice and warm, Ben said, you're a good friend.

Ethan smiled to himself. You're a good friend too. I'm glad you consider me as a friend now.

They were in Ethan's bedroom now. He had string lights draped across the room, tediously taped to the walls where the paint peeled slightly. The two of them sat on the floor, backs against the bed watching The Devil All the Time.

Ben's eyes wandered from the film on TV.

This thing is scaring the shit out of me, can we turn it off?

Ethan laughed. Sure, he said and switched it off.

Sorry I didn't write back to you this week, by the way.
That's quite alright, Ethan said, and understandable despite well, you know, your illness. Actually, if you don't want to write letters at all, that's fine.
Ben seemed a little confused. Why do you say that? Your letters are the highlight of my day, mostly.
Ethan felt a warm glow ignite within him. Oh, well—that's very kind of you. That's also the case when I read your letters, but I think it might be cringe-worthy if I want just like 'yeah, me too, your letters are the highlight of my day too'.
Ben was laughing at him now. He put his hand on Ethan's shoulder and said: that's basically what you just said anyway!

Yeah, I did to be fair. It's true though!

Is it really? Ben teased. Well, I'm glad we feel the same way.
That sounds weirdly romantic, Ethan said. And they both laughed.

Ethan.

I received your gift in the mail today, an edition of The Pickwick Papers! Why didn't you say anything in college? You're that secretive kinda person I'm starting to figure, eh? Thank you, I mean it. There's nothing more valuable than the gifting of stories.

The other night, round yours, I looked over at you as we switched on the film and the opening credits were rolling, and you had a tear in your eye. It may have been a trick of the light, but I swear, I saw it, a tear, just one. Sorry if this sounds invasive, it's just at the time I didn't know what to say or how to address it. Was something up? Anything going on? I just don't want you to ever feel you can't talk to me.

B.

Dear Ben,

From Afar

You catch my eye,
and I turn to look
in your direction.

Even against the
cerulean sky,
your eyes glisten.

I try to be subtle,
not being so blatant
that you notice me.

But you do,
and the eye contact
is brief.

I say something
to you in that moment,
but I'm not sure

You quite catch it,

Like with you my eye was caught.

Ethan x

Ethan.

Wait…is that your poetry?
You're so fucking cool.

B.

Dear Ben,

To answer your question, yes, that is my poetry. Simply put, I sent it to you as I was still trying to compose my response to your question about the tear your saw in my eye.
May I say, I appreciate how we use these letters to tell each other about stuff we're not quite ready to say face-to-face yet. Even though we've had some deep conversations in-person, still, some things are difficult to get out verbally without becoming tongue-tied. Seems writing is the answer to that.

The tear in my eye (which I thought I had successfully concealed) was a hint of emotional joy and slight overwhelm seeping out from inside of me. It's been longer than I can remember since someone has considered me a true, real friend, and vice versa. Your kindness is valued more than you'll ever imagine. I don't think I ever really knew what true friendship felt like until now. And in that moment, it made me emotional. The 'friend-ish friendships' I've had in the past have felt restraining, not completely real. I've had to hide parts of myself to remain 'a friend'. Nobody has ever really seen the actual me, until you. How I am around you is how I…*am.*

Ethan x

Ethan.

Your previous letter was really kind. Likewise, by the way!
I'm glad that you trust me enough to even consider chatting about
that kind of stuff.

Alas, the holidays are coming up, and so are our plans.

B.

THREE WEEKS LATER

Ethan.

I am aware that, despite your excitement for our camping trip, its not really your thing…

So, in an attempt to help you—seems we're not seeing each other in college every day now, I have enclosed my 'non-essential' packing list. I know you are intelligent enough to figure out what essentials you need to bring!
Also, I should mention that I've got you a gift, and I really hope you like it.

See you soonnnn!!!!!

B.

Non-Essentials:

Ethan's kindly gifted edition of THE PICKWICK PAPERS *(would consider essential, but technically it's not)*
Marshmallows to cook on fire
Ethan's gift!!!
Polaroid camera + extra film
Laptop for Netflix
Spare warm clothing
e-Reader
Glasses
Alcohol (would ALSO consider essential, but technically it's not)

Dear Ben,

Thank you for considering me INTELLIGENT! And also for your enclosed list of supposed 'non-essentials'.

I'm writing this the night before we leave, so most likely, you'll be reading this letter right in-front of me, or when we get home in a couple of days.

God, I'm just imagining what it's going to be like! Sunsets, the sounds of nature, music, books…
It'll be wonderful, you know? I'm sure you do.
You're right, by the way, about the outdoors not really being my forte, but I'm up for giving this camping in the wilderness thing a go. With you I am, anyways. And aww, what are you like? Going about, getting me gifts! No need, really, though I do look forward to seeing what it is.

This evening, whist I was packing, I listened to *Seventeen Going Under* on my record player. There's this song where it mentions bullies bleeding you dry, kind of hit hard, you know. But there was one line that stuck with me. *'It breaks you up'*. I was like…fucking hell, that's so true. When I was being bullied, mostly verbally in my case, it really does break you up. Bit by bit, comment by comment, sneer after sneer, breaking you just a fragment more each time. When it gets really bad, you're just a pile of ash, tiny, broken up pieces of what was once there, and it's incredibly difficult to put yourself back together, and even when and if you manage to, you'll never be the same. The truth is, you'll actually lose pieces of yourself in the process, and you can't get them back. If only people realized the detrimental affects they can have on others. Scary stuff.

If you ever felt this way, I'm really sorry you had to go through that, too.

I'm all packed up now, anyway. Tried not to bring too much, just a duffel bag sized thingy. Thingy, huh? I never use that sort of vocab. Maybe your way of words is rubbing off on me.

Ethan x

Dear Ben,

I'm writing to you only a few minutes after I've finished the previous one!
Seems you enjoyed the last one, I've attached another poem for you to read if you're bored at any point. Like the previous one, it's the original copy, ripped from my notebook, so I hope you keep it safe.

Ethan x

...On One Looking Through Me (Specifically Through Me)

Am I an asset belonging to a museum?
Am I sitting proudly in a glass case?
so when you take a photograph,
the flash obscures your vision of me.

Stop looking through me like I'm an object.
I'm here,
and you know that.
I'll look up eventually and you'll avert your gaze

as quick as can be.

So hurry now, look away
before our eyes meet.

When Ethan arrived at Ben's house on the second day of half term break,
he came with a duffel bag and a coat draped over his arm. The air was
crisp, and the weather was due to be nice the next couple of days.
How's it going? Ben said, bringing Ethan into a hug. Feels like I haven't
seen you in ages!

Two days, Ethan laughed.

You ready?
Excuse me? Yes! Of course I'm ready. Are we leaving now, like straight
away?

Nah, give it half an hour, make sure we're all sorted.

Alright.

Got everything?

Hope so.
Ah! Your little gift, Ben wafted his hand in a forward direction, follow me!

Oh, wow! Are we actually going to your room?
Right, yeah, ignore the mess.
Can't be as bad as last time, you outright refused we venture up there,
Ethan joked.
Ben placed his hand on Ethan's shoulder and said: I was just being

mysterious.

Ethan raised his eyebrow. Very funny, he replied.

Ben's room was dimly lit by his retro-looking desk lamp. A large assortment of battered classic novels were scattered across the floor. There were some ripped out pages from old, useless editions which had black marker blacking out lots of the words.

What! Ethan exclaimed, you do blackout poetry?
Oh, er, wait! Ben hurried to pick up the discarded pages off the floor in an attempt to hide them.

You said I was cool...

You are!

But this! Holy shit Ben, let me see!

Nah, you don't want to see that. He laughed subtly.

Come on, please. Ethan looked hopeful.
Ben's lips curled into a slight smile as he said: Right, fine. Hang on. Flicking between all the loose pages, trying to find one to show Ethan. Ah, he said, this one's alright I suppose. And he handed it to Ethan.

~~I can listen no longer in silence. I must speak to~~ **you** ~~by such means as~~ **are within my** ~~reach. You pierce my~~ **soul. I am** ~~half agony, half hope. Tell me not that I am too late, that such precious feelings are gone for ever. I offer myself to you again with~~ **a heart** ~~even more your own than when~~ **you almost** **broke** ~~it, eight years and a half ago. Dare not say that man forgets sooner than woman, that his love has an earlier death. I have loved none but you. Unjust I may have been, weak and resentful I have been, but never inconstant. You alone have brought me to Bath. For you alone, I think and plan. Have you not seen this? Can you fail to have understood my~~ **wishes? I had** ~~not waited even these ten days, could I have read~~ **your feelings, as I** ~~think you must~~ **have** ~~penetrated mine. I can hardly write. I am every instant hearing something which overpowers me. You sink your voice, but I can distinguish the tones of that voice when they would be~~ **lost** ~~on others. Too good, too excellent creature! You do us justice, indeed.~~ **You** ~~do believe that there is true attachment and constancy among men.~~

~

There's not many people why drive at seventeen, I don't think. Ethan said as the car engine sputtered to life. He held in his hands a framed extract from The Pickwick Papers. What a charming gift.

Really? I thought it were pretty normal. No?

Mmm. Maybe you're right then.

Can you teach me how to do blackout poetry?

Can you teach me how to write poetry?

Stop answering questions with questions!

Why?

God! You're doing it again!

I know, Ben smirked, but yes, I can.

Ben moved off the driveway as Ethan plugged his phone into the sound system in the car. He played Talking Heads.
Ben accelerated into fourth gear, glanced at Ethan and said: Old-school, huh?

You got it, Ethan replied.

During the drive there, the two of them had a few general conversations about college, but just listened to the music for the most part. A comforting silence. Soon enough, the houses were no longer repetitive and terraced, but sparse and cottage-like. The road narrowed and the hills began to emerge, rolling throughout the landscape, the mountains emitted their sweet, crisp air, welcoming you in. The long grass swished as the car passed it, the sun peeking through the wispy clouds, suspended low.

It wasn't long until the car came to a stop after Ben pulled into a small gravel car park just off the road. There was a faint path that led into a grassy area, and down a hill.

Ben turned off the engine, let out a satisfied sigh and said: There!

Are we here?

Yeah. Beautiful drive that, wasn't it.

Wasn't it just.
Ethan grabbed his own water bottle and handed a fresh one to Ben. Here's to two days of tranquility!

Once they had set up their tents, Ethan asked: Is this, like—legal?
Bit late now, isn't it? Ben joked.

I know, but is it?

Yeah it is. You worry a lot. It's a wild camping area.

Alright then. And yeah, I worry a lot. Sorry.
What for?

For worrying a lot.
Chill.

~

The sunset cast a fire red haze across the horizon, and as the light faded, the first night was upon them and the darkness drew in. Unlike at home, they could see many stars because there was less light pollution. It was beautiful. Ethan could have swore one of them glistening crystals met his gaze. Just for a moment.

They sat in the blue-dark.

Thanks, Ben said.

For what?
Just, you know, this. He gestured at nothing in-particular. This, bond we have, where we are, the letters. Just, thanks.
Ethan felt a lump in his throat. Thank you, too, he said.

NINE WEEKS LATER

Ethan.

I've been reminiscing on our little getaway. We didn't do much, but in a good way, if that makes any sense. It was just us and nature.

I miss it.
But it's DECEMBER. Basically Christmas, right?
And we're off.

The other day, on our last one of the term, you cried, remember? I don't mean to remind you for bad reason, I just want to know you are okay. You got called a faggot and it tipped you over the edge. I got home and cried as well. For you and for the sake of my, your— *our* anger.
Even though the mood was cold, you were warm. I could feel your warmth against me. Did you feel my warmth against you? It's been a week or so…

Please come over?

B.

Dear Ben,

Yes, I'll come over. I would really like that.

See you tomorrow.

Ethan x

Ethan.

As I'm writing this, you've just left my house. Said you had to be home for tea. Pretty sure you said you'll come back in the morning; the day went so fast. I'll post it through your letter box tonight on my way to the corner shop.

I would like to re-live it. If you get bored at any point, feel free to stop reading and discard this letter.

You arrived at like eleven in the morning. It was a really cold day, but the type where the sun is out, yet the air is ice cold, bitter. You came in and—as promised, I made us brunch. You said it was lovely, and I'm glad you liked it.

Following this we went for a walk in the chill outside, stopping by at a café to get a hot chocolate.
By the time we got home, our beverages were surprisingly still warm to finish off, and we did so whilst talking over the early daytime television shows.

A few hours later, I forced you to watch *Arthur Christmas* (I know you didn't like it, but I still strongly believe it is the best Christmas film…ever). I sat on the left side of the sofa, and you were kind of lying down, your legs resting over mine. Without really thinking, I began fiddle with the seams of your joggers. What are you doing? You mumbled to me, smiling faintly. I don't know, I replied, honestly. I think the truth is, I just wanted to touch you. Is that weird? I'm sorry. It's just, I said I'd always be honest with you. I must of fell asleep after that, because I woke up to you lightly tapping my shoulder. Ben, you said. Hey, you've been asleep for like an hour. I apologized, but you said it was fine, and excuse to watch something other than *Arthur Christmas.*

I like you, Ben Mathews, I really do.

B. x

Dear Ben,

CAN YOU BELIEVE IT? IT WAS SNOWING TODAY!
I'm sitting at my desk facing the window watching the little flakes
of soft, soft ice lightly flail and float gracefully to the ground.

Today, today, today. I can't get it out of my head. Your parents
weren't in, so they didn't notice I was at yours two days in a row.
Who'd have thought we'd have a snow day this close to Christmas?
Not me, that's for sure.

I digress, but I loved reading about our day in your last letter (which
was delivered very promptly!), and so I thought I'd have a go, too.

Our conversation when we sat down with a cup of coffee was (from
what I recall) as follows:
I told you: I got your letter.
Ah, I'm glad it didn't disintegrate when I put it through the letter
box.
Very funny.
I am, you said. And you laughed then.
I like you, too.
You blushed and said: Good, yeah. Cool—I'm glad.
No, like *like* you.
Oh.
You said you wanted an excuse to touch me, I thought we may feel
the same way?
No, it's just. Well...
What's up, Ben?
No, nothing...just. Fuck. Fucking hell Ethan. You caught me off
guard there, is all.
Ah. Sorry. I'm sorry. I'm still your best friend. I'm sorry.

No, Ethan! Stop talking.
Sorry.
Stop apologizing.
Sorry. God—errrm. Ok, yeah.

Then you stood up and gave me a hug. I could hear you crying a
little.
You looked me right in the eyes and softly pressed your forehead
against mine.

I said that you were giving me mixed signals.
I'm just really overwhelmed, you said.
That's okay. We're okay.

I swear in that moment, you were going to kiss me, but your lips
just about touched mine, and slowly, you moved away.

After a tense silence, you started laughing through your tears.
We like each other, you said.
I guess, I said, smiling now.
I really like you.
Thanks.
Can you tell me you like me? I just want to be sure.
Yeah, I like you, a lot. I really do.

At this point, I hadn't even taken my coat off, and you asked if we
should go out in the snow. You put on *your* coat, and we went to
the local park.

The snow crunched as we walked over it, each flake that landed on
me felt like a kiss from nature. And then there was an ice cold down
my back. You'd thrown a lump of snow at me.

Ey! I shouted as you ran off.

I chased you with a snowball now, I threw it and missed.

Too bad, Ethe! You shouted at me when I ran past you.

You caught up with me and jumped on my back. I'm not sure how strong you thought I was, but I couldn't hold you, so we both fell onto the ground, you on top of me.

Ethe? I joked. Is that my new name, Ethe?

Is that okay, you asked.

Say it again!

No, cause now you're taking the piss.

Nah, go on. Say it again!

Ethe, I really like you.

And I laughed. You are hilarious, Ben.

I tried to sit up out of the snow, but you lay on top of me. We wrestled in the sea of white. Finally you came out on top, so you rested on me, chest on chest, nose touching mine. In that beautiful moment, you leaned into me slowly and kissed me. I laughed against your lips. A little breathless, I told you I'd never properly kissed anyone before.

That's okay, you told me, and leaned in again.

It was sweet, as your lips traced mine. You were soft and gentle, as we lay there in the snow.

When we parted, you lay next to me, reached for my hand, held it, and we watched the snowflakes fall around us.

Ethan x

ONE WEEK LATER

Hello?

Ben said when he answered the phone. It was late. He sat up in bed.
Ben? Said Ethan's voice down the phone. His voice was faint and shaky.
Yeah? You good?
Can you come and help me? Please?
Ethan? What's happened? Are you hurt?
I'm bleeding. It's dark, Ben. Please, I need you.

Without a second thought, Ben switched on his bedside light, pulled on some clothes that were discarded beside the bed and ran downstairs, out the door.
Where are you Ethan? I'm coming, okay. Where are you?
The street next to mine. I don't know what it's—
I'm coming, okay. Stay on the line, I'm in the car.

When he was pulling out of the driveway, his mum came to the door.
Ben! What are you doing? Jesus Christ! What are you—

Mum, Ben shouted out the car window, it's fine, okay. I'll be home soon.

Ben, for God's sake lad! Where are you going?

*But he was already driving away. The roads were a little icy.
When he was near Ethan's house, he turned down the nearest street. He
was there, on the pavement. The streetlights were orange and dim.*

*Ethan! He said, getting out of the car, running over.
Ethan's head was leaning up against a fence. His face was bloody, and his
jeans were frayed at the knee. A trail of blood ran from his nose down*

onto his shirt.

Fuck. Fucking hell Ethan.

*But Ethan didn't talk. He just sobbed.
What happened? Talk to me! Ben said, touching his cheek with his thumb.*

*Please, talk to me.
The ones from school. I was out with Casey and that lot, just in town. I was
walking home, and the ones from school saw me. I tried to keep my head*

down, but they crossed the road. Followed me.

*They had followed him, one stepping forward to pull him back by the
collar.
Would you look who it is? The sissy from school, the boy said. This
brought with it an onslaught of laughter from the others behind him. He
pulled Ethan towards him by his shirt. Someone's looking real manly
tonight, he said. And he smoothed his finger over Ethan's eye lids and
looked at the glittery remnants of eyeshadow.*

Get the fuck off me, Ethan said calmly.

Get off me! Get off me, the boy mocked.

Ethan was too afraid to move, but he tried to edge away a little.

Where you off to then?

*Just home.
Ah! Home, how cute.
Ethan tried his very best to fight it, but he had welled up, and if he*

*blinked, a tear would fall down his face, meander through his features.
We won't give up pestering you until you act like a normal lad. You've got
the learn these things.
And there it was, the tear.*

I mean, look at the state of you. What a little queer.
Ethan tried to run now, down the street. He ran, tripping along the dark
pavement.
Come back here fag, another of the boys shouted now as they caught him
up. They grabbed him by the hair and punched his face, and again, again,
again. They floored him and kicked at his sides until he was sobbing and
bloody.
Piece of shit. Pull yourself together, poof!
The boys walked away as if nothing had happened. One at the back stood
above him for a second, spat, and said: Fucking gays.

And here he was, with Ben, who held him tight for a few minutes, before
helping him up and leading him to the passenger seat of the car. The
engine was still running, the headlights on.
It's okay. You're safe now. It's okay.
Ethan wiped his eyes with the back of his hand. Sorry, he mumbled.
You have absolutely nothing to be sorry for, alright? You're safe now.
You're safe now.

~

When they got back to Ben's house, Ethan called his mum, told her what
had happened, where he was now, he was safe. She was going to pick him
up from Ben's. But don't rush, Ethan told her, nothing more will happen,
I'm okay now, everything will be okay.

Ben's mum came downstairs, a face like thunder, she was about to ask
where Ben had been, why he ignored her, where he had gone at such a
time. But then she saw Ethan, hunched over on a chair in the kitchen. Ben
placed a cup of tea in front of him.
Jesus, Ethan, what happened? She hurried over and pulled up a chair next
to him.
And he told her.

Sometimes, in life, we walk down the wrong path, just by chance, and
come across things we would never have expected. We find ourselves in

terrible situations. But other times we are free, and it is beautiful. Freedom —when you have it, is beautiful. Take that freedom with gusto, run with it, because at any moment the path you run along could lead you astray.

I feel limp, I ache. I feel frail.

I am a fire out of fuel. I am a single ember. That's all that's left of me.

Stamp on me and extinguish the last of my hope.

What's the point if I can't live a life free of those who want to extinguish the last of my hope?

There's always a point, he would say. And that's what makes me, a single ember, burn just a little brighter. Still though, I am ever so close to fading away.

-        From Ethan Walker's Diary.

PART TWO
LIVE WELL

Ethan.

I know you're hurting right now.
If you let yourself feel the pain, when it's ready, it'll wash over.
Don't suppress it. Feel it. Don't make yourself a void of emotion.
If you feel it, you can move on easier.

I left some warm cookies at your house last night. Your dad
asked if I wanted to head upstairs and see you, but I thought you
might want some space.

If it makes you feel better at all, my mum said you should come
spend Christmas at ours, bring your parents. It's up to you
though.

Look after yourself.

B. x

Dear Ben,

Sorry I haven't written to you for a few days, but I took your advice. Did you make those cookies, they were so nice.

I'm starting to feel more myself again, slowly but surely. I think I need to see you. I really want to see you, and I would love to spend Christmas at yours. I think my parents like the idea too, it's usually just the three of us, so it'll be something a bit different. Ah, just imagine it. God, that thought has cheered me up.

Can you come round tomorrow? Nobody is in. I want to see you.

Ethan x

Ethan.

The minute I stepped inside your house today, you hugged me tight.

It felt comforting to see you again, and it felt normal. Things had returned to normal.

We sat on your bed and talked for hours. Then you leaned into me and started kissing me. You seemed to ask permission with your eyes. Yes, yes, yes. Softly, you tugged at my shirt with your index finger and thumb.
Yeah?
Only if you want to.
Yes. Yes. And you whispered in my ear, yes.
You pulled off your shirt, I helped you. And then mine, you helped me. We continued removing our clothes. Warm skin against warm skin.
You said: Can you kiss me? Can I touch you?
It was slow, almost awkward, but not in a bad way. It just *was*, and that was fine. We took our time. We were entangled now, it got more intense, we were breathing heavily. We were going to go further, but you couldn't. You started crying, saying, I'm sorry, I'm sorry, I just don't want this.
No, no, *I'm* sorry, I said. I lay beside you then. We were comfortable there.
Don't be sorry, you said, it's me. God—fuck. Sorry Ben.
Did I do something?
No, no. I just don't think. I don't think I want sex, like proper sex.
Ok, alright. Why?
I can't explain it. It makes me—I don't know, it makes me want to be sick.

Oh.

It's not you! It's not, that's just—that's just the way I am, how I feel. I don't know if that will ever change.

Are you nervous?

No, I should have said, I think I'm—I think I'm asexual.

That's okay, don't worry.

Like I'm into you, a lot, I just don't want sex, but I wouldn't want it with anyone. You don't have a stay with me or anything…

I let you cry, lay on my side and kissed your forehead. Is this okay?

Yeah, yeah, I like that. Can we stay like this?

I nodded. We'll figure things out, I said.

We will figure things out, you know. Don't feel bad. Please don't feel bad. You're my best friend Ethan, well, I'm pretty sure we're a lot more than that.

B. x

Dear Ben,

Thank you for the understanding, and I know you'll tell me not to apologize but I'm sorry. I just didn't know how to tell you.

There's a Christmas market in town, I was wondering if you would like to go?

Ethan x

The Christmas market was packed. Ethan and Ben met at the local library. The air was cold but warm with cheer and liveliness.
Hey, Ben said as he walked over to Ethan, who waved back at him and smiled.
Should we get eggnog?

Yes, that'd be lush, Ben replied.
That's what they did. The stall had a sweet but spicy aroma, steam wafted out of the serving window, and the staff were all dressed in matching red hoodies. They thanked the kind lady who served them at the stall and ventured into the market with their warm beverages. Ethan sipped it and felt the liquid travel through his cold body, it glowed inside of him. Ben laced his fingers in between Ethan's, and they strolled amongst the Christmas trees, carol singers, the string lights draped across the street arranged in a zigzag pattern. The main tree at the center of the market glittered in the evening moonlight. The lights on it danced in all their vibrancy. Baubles and other decorations swayed lightly in the frosty breeze.
They sat down on a bench up close to the tree.

We can come to yours for Christmas, by the way, Ethan said.

Yes! Oh my God, it's going to be so good! Ben replied and put his arm around Ethan's shoulders, pulled him in close.

Ben?

Yeah?

You know you said we're a lot more than best friends?

We are.

Like, yeah—obviously, Ethan said and laughed. I just wanted to say, I appreciate you, a lot. For everything. I think, wait—can we class ourselves as...

Wait! Can I say it?

You don't know what I'm going to say.

I think I do.

Go on, okay.

Boyfriends? He paused and then continued, I thought that'd be romantic, but it was so fucking cringeworthy!

That's all part of the fun.

Fair comment, yeah. But holy shit, I'm Ethan Walker's boyfriend!

You are really quite funny, Ben Mathews, Ethan said, laughing.

~

On Christmas day, Ethan and his parents arrived at Ben's house around one in the afternoon. Bruce the Jack Russel was very happy to see these mysterious people in his house, it seemed.

Hiya, how are we? We haven't spoke in a while, Ethan's mum said as they entered the house.

Ah well, you know it gets hectic this time of the year, Ben's mum replied, come here love, give me a hug.

Ben gave Ethan a look as if to say: mums eh?

The two dads just kind of smiled and gave each other and the boys a tap on the back.

How very masculine of you, Ben joked at his dad. Going to give the women a little kiss on the cheeks as well?

Yes actually, now you've said it, I will, his dad replied like he was proving a point. He guided Ben into the dining room by his shoulders and continued: Also, since when has my masculinity been a way for you to poke fun at me?

Well, you know, Ben gave him a teasing look.

After the dinner, they sat in the living room. The fire was crackling, warming the room. Everyone was squeezed onto the two sofas and playing some kind of game. They had paper crowns on, and interacted with each other dramatically.

The lights of the Christmas tree lit up the wall around it, a colorful glow.

Ben nudged Ethan and said: Back in a minute.
They both left and ran up the stairs. On the bed were two gifts, wrapped very differently.

Here, Ethan said, handing Ben his gift.
He unwrapped it carefully. Inside was a photo of the two of them on the snowy day at the park, they were laying on the ground laughing. In the bottom corner was a poem titled 'From Afar'. It was one he had sent Ben a while back. He had a tear in his eye.
That poem, Ethan said, it was about you.

PART THREE
I'LL NEVER FORGET THE TIME I SPENT WITH YOU

SPRING

Dear Ben,

College/school (I have a tendency to call it school even though it is in fact, technically, college). I digress, but college has been difficult lately, avoiding the bullies and all that. Thank you for helping me. I'm also glad that you convinced me to start therapy. It's slowly beginning to change the way I think about things, and I've found I'm driving myself insane with miniscule details of an interaction a little less than usual.

I'm just thinking back to the other day when we went to the park, and the flowers were beginning to bloom, the trees were getting greener, the scent of Spring rain wrapped around us. We sat on a blanket and ate a picnic. When we got back to my house, I went and got the pajamas I bought you as a gift because I thought you would like them, which you did. We sat and watched a film and decided to stay over. You slept in my bed with me.

In the morning, you were awake and showered by the time I woke up. You had no clean clothes with you, so I got some out of my wardrobe. A pair of shorts and a sweatshirt, everything else would have been a little too small. I quite like seeing you in my clothes, I'm not sure why.

Ethan x

Ethan.

Where would we be right now without each other?

B. x

SIX WEEKS LATER

Dear Ben,

We watched the sunset last night. Lay on our backs on top of a hill not far from your house. You held my hand and played beautifully calm music on your phone.

The sky glistened.

You're a shooting star, you whispered in my ear.
You're a shooting star.

Ethan x

Ethan.

You've taught me so much about myself, and so much about the
world.
The year we've spent together seems like a lifetime, like you've
always been there, a constant in my life from the very beginning.
When you mentioned that line from a song 'it breaks you up', it has
stuck with me. I feel like we've both helped one another piece each
other back together. Whatever may have happened in our lives
before we met began to heal from the minute we started talking.

Remember one of our first conversations about Emily Dickinson?
The first day of college.
We're both applying for universities soon enough. Not the same
ones. How do you think we will be living apart for such a long
stretch? We spend a lot of our time together, and I don't think my
love for that will ever fade. I'll miss your warmth, and the comfort
of your presence.

B. x

AND AFTER...

Ethan.

As I finished my packing for university, I thought about you. I thought about us.
I know you keep saying how much you'll miss me, how much I'll miss you, but please make me a promise…
Enjoy it, live in the very moment. I can imagine you typing away in your English Literature lectures, pissing about with your flat-mates, frantically stressing over essay deadlines. And I know, you'll be having the time of your life. All you've talked about for so long is how wonderful uni is going to be. So please, just live it. For me. Don't yearn for us to be together, because we will be soon enough.

This is the final letter I'll write you before I get to my uni, so I wanted to remind you, just as I did when we watched sunset on the hill…

Hell, Ethan, you're a shooting star!

Love Ben x

Dear Ben,

I'm leaving for half term break a few days early because I have some
party for my cousins to attend. But it's been so long, Ben, so long.
I kept the promise. I took each day as it came, and the times I
allowed the visions of you and me together to sneak in, they
flooded my heart with warmth and nostalgia and joy.

Love Ethan x

Ethan.

As our break drew to a close, the both of us packed up ready to head back to uni.
You stopped by my house to say goodbye, but didn't have time to come in. So I met you on the street, just outside the gate. We didn't exchange many words, because our emotions had their own conversation. You brought me into a hug. As we parted, you smiled, but I could see the melancholy hidden below it.
Our arms were outstretched as we held hands, just with the tips of our fingers. Once again, we turned and went our separate ways.

Your parents invited me round for tea the evening we get back, so you bet, I'll be here, always, ready to welcome you home.

Love Ben x

SELECTED POETRY
& VIGNETTES

OFF CENTRE THEATRICS

I

It was me who set the stage just off-centre.

II

I let my makeup brush caress my cheek
like I was my own lover.
The brush was the notion of my love,
because of course I would never have a lover,
and so me and my makeup brush;
we got along well.

The double vision that affected the lights
all around the mirror
was wild.

The bulbs split and dipped in and out of each other,
circling
oscillating
and morphing once more.

I had done this show many times now,
and I was never quite right.

I have never been quite right.

I come off stage every time,
aching limbs,
creaking bones,

delicate and frail,
like at any moment I would stretch out my leg
and it would snap.

Like a damned door,
my hinges squeal at their use.
Bolts in my brain, loose.
I am an object of performance.

The audience fix their eyes upon me,
and I owe them
and for every mistake I make
I shall be forever indebted.

Help me for I am drowning
in lights and bodies.

Even the stage rigs watch me,
their eyes nestled in the struts,
in the cross-sections of welding
vast across the auditorium.

Obnoxious little girls screech and squawk
at my pirouettes.
My
                        twists,
                                twirls,
                    and
            whirls
delight the front-rowers
who bagged their tickets

months prior.

The wrinkled man,
selling
my
face in
his
box office.
   To him I was a number
   and a ticket
   and a twenty-quid note.

   My face more notorious than the Queen's
   as there are more tickets for the show
   than tenner notes.

III

I'm performing,
crying
  PASSION
 because I'm like a
   wind

         up
    D O L L
one ticket
one twist
and it's almost as if I am the stage itself
and my determination deforms it
and as I jolt my body around,
the lighting rigs creak
and they're going to fall

and I will be well-lit no more.

The
          stage is shaking
                    and the   orchestra
musicians are screaming
                              the theatre has always
     owned

                                                            me
and this
                         is the
          end of it
                         all.
the audience
     rush   out
of   their seats
                         as the
                                   stage   reveals

     legs,
thick steel
     struts to
               us   all.

The makeup

     removed...   THIS IS WHAT I AM.

they better
     warn

               the ticket   man

in the
    box   office
                  that
tHe
woMan
On
thE
ticKet
desiGn
dOesn't
loOk
The
sAme
anYmore.

her   eyes
   are   spotlights.

WE LAY, I FEAR

I

hold on
you said,
as we make
our way
to the bed.

you are suddenly
a stranger
to
me.

anxiety struck,
we were about to fuck,
and now there is a
stranger in
my room.

I think:
fuck!
not *me,*
but off!

you were my lover
and now your presence
sets
me on

                  e

                       d

                             g

                                  e

you smile,
playful.

what's wrong?

then you're on me,
not *on*
on me,
just comforting.

it's scary.

unknown,
oblivion.

"
      maybe it's just a phase. "

II

we lay entangled on your sofa,
calm hearing and feeling the steadiness
of your breath.

out the window,
the city lives on.

lights of polluting traffic,
bright billboards blinding pedestrians,
shop signs,
night clubs,
lights those urban photographers use their
long exposure
on.

        get vast, sweeping images,
            a motion
            (emotion)
                    to the trails of light.

and now we are
a   fragment of that light,
leaving a
                trail of hope in our wake.

IS THIS HOW IT'S GOING TO BE NOW?

your shadow dominates the corridors/your is you/is not singular/is
you as in/them/the group/I'm late for my lesson/cringing/head
down/slow stroll/hope you leave/of course you don't/why would
you care about being on time for your lesson/thinking I passed
you/head up/safety of the teachers voice/in the doorway/sorry can
I get past/you can look at me when you talk/I look up/*wheeeeeeey*/
they jeer/like you have control of me/do you fancy me then/or any
of the lads/and I stutter/nah/did he expect any less deciding to be
all gay in school/drop it/please/he even talks gay/squeeze past/
warmth of the body feels cold on me/coldness of pointless hatred/
wonder what door I'll find them at/next/maybe the other them's/or
these/them/those/that group/ah/this is my favourite lesson/

It's three in the morning. My desk lamp is creating a dim, warm glow in the corner of my dorm. It's one of those—our old friend: the Sleepless Night. Gets me at least once per fortnight. With these nights comes an overactive brain, and tonight's thought is: fuck the system. The system that whittles our worth, intelligence, value down to an hour, two hours. The system that says: you're not capable because you crack under my pressure; when in fact we are all perfectly capable, and we excel! The old, straight white guy who points his finger and says: you'll do this my way, my right answers, my criteria, and you're damn worthless because I lack care and empathy and your life will be determined by my narrow-minded system that will try it's very best to vigorously mould you into the person I and society desires. Oh, don't be silly, they would never admit such a thing! You must do this, you must be this, you must look, talk, walk like this. You must follow this restrictive policy and that restrictive policy, this pointless rule, this perfectly curated structure. You must, you must, you must. You must live like this, you must nod you head and accept my nit-picking, you must hide yourself, hang your head in shame because you're a man and you fucked another man, you must wear this so you all blend into one like some strange morphing of bodies, you can't do this, you can't do that. You must live, laugh, love, but not love who you want because some bigots might not like it, you must conform to this, conform to that because you're a puppet and I'm your puppeteer! You must express yourself, but not too much. You must not say this, agree with this, disagree with that, speak like *this* because you're a puppet and I'm your ventriloquist. I'm the puppeteer who can't keep to myself, and you are a puppet.

Oh no, don't cry!

SHOALS

Surface distant,
thoughts present.

Fragments of interaction,
specks of dust,
float, flail, form as scales.

Glimmer,
faces appear, memories dissipate,
ebb and flow.

Such is true,
enveloped in the endless Blue.

Shoals of sea creature,
Deep dips of emotion,
observe with sentiment
for them, one has sweet devotion.

Nothing matters in this
deep ocean.

LOST BOY
(from a *you're not the only one* sequel: *we are young*)

A slight breeze caught a pale orange leaf and carried it though the
air.
It drifted across the edge of a boy's periphery and upon landing,
found a place nestled between the blades of grass.

George watched the leaves fall,
one after another,
witnessing the beginning of his eighteenth autumn.

This was his favourite season,
and it brought comfort
that eased the nerves of moving to university,
just a bit,
like a steaming mug of soup
after a walk through town in the bitter air.

Moving to university was something that George found exciting,
a new horizon,
the sunset peaking over the hill;
but it would be a lie if he said the nerves,
the thought of it didn't keep him up at night before the move.

There's suddenly this huge distance between him
and home,
and although the thought makes him giddy,
it in equal measure,
brings a sickly feeling to his stomach.

To start a life somewhere entirely new

at eighteen is quite a
daunting prospect.

He can't decide how he does feel,
or how he should feel.
Its all one big cocktail of emotions,
and he just wishes he could share them with his friends back home.

Archie,
confused about his future and working in the meantime,
and Elijah,
pursuing his love for writing,
both took a gap year.
And Leo,
he's still stuck in college,
being a year younger than the rest of them.

But this is it,
the start of something new,
and it's going to be wonderful.

/

His room is nothing much at the moment.

There is the odd box on the floor,
bursting, tape clinging on
for dear life.

Clothes,
some folded,
but mostly in heaps.

His parents helped as much as they could,
but in a single day,
as well as eating lunch out—
there just isn't enough time.
So this is what's left.

When his parents left,
there was a slight emptiness.
To the room,
and the light,
the way it spilled through the curtains
in a tone a little less warm,
and in George himself.
A silence that brewed,
a space, but an opportunity,
begging to be fulfilled.

Work hard, be nice.
Uh-huh, okay.
A smile.
And the door clicked shut.

WHY DOES THIS PEN OF MINE ALWAYS FIND ANGER?

I've come to find
that we spend our time
doing things because others
want us to.

Your policy
and groupings
of bodies,
personalities.
     My time isn't yours
     for the taking,
          and yet I still find you
          chipping away at it.
I'm baffled by those
who can't see all this
for what it is:
the churning of little cogs
in their
     machine.

Who are you
if entirely ruled over
by other people?

-June '22: 23.01

POST-GATHERING

How do you explain a feeling
that seems like
it shouldn't be real?
          or doesn't deserve to exist?

What does and doesn't deserve a place in your mind?

          The paranoia:
The great enjoyment I feel to be
surrounded by Them,
spend time with Them.

But the feeling isn't mutual,
          tell yourself the feeling isn't mutual!

It ended so fast,
I was an empty shell,
come
          and
                    go.

To try so hard,
and always be left feeling this way.
One way   <<>>   or another

What defines a friendship,
one down, two down.
          As if with friendship, you shouldn't ever feel this way,
     friendship itself
is impossible.

IT BREAKS YOU UP: AN UNSEEN LETTER

Dear Ben,

Today I watched the swift decent of cherry blossoms, saw the leaves of evergreen trees ruffle in delight, and I thought of you.

We're in our second year of university now, and from being so caught up in the tribulations that come with that, our letters have been short, rare, a treat. I've missed writing to you, but I simply haven't the time, and I'll always remember what you said, and what I had promised that time: don't yearn for the past or what is back home, because I'd waited so long for this moment, university, so just live. Live. So I have. Occasionally, I've been strolling around campus and thought I saw you—which of course I didn't, but you're always there in the back of my mind, keeping my conscience company.

It's been a long time, Ben. The last time I saw you was half term of our first year, and since then everything's been a blur. I could say it's gone by fast, but when I remember having our conversation over dinner that night, it seems like an eternity has passed. We've been in this ocean for so long. But rather than the currents pulling us further and further from each other, we've just been treading water, waiting for the tides to change and we feel the pull, the urge. I feel that now. Do you? The workload is dying down for a short while, and that's our sign. Put our lives on hold and reunite.

Ethan x

DEAR ALL COTTON WOOL SPINSTERS,

I call you bunch of folk by this blanket term due to your nature. A
nature to painstakingly control everyone and everything. You and
your little pincers, tit-for-tat, this and that.

Dear all Cotton Wool Spinsters,

I encourage you all to wake up, see the world and the souls within it
through the eyes of Trust.

Dear all Cotton Wool Spinsters,

I wish you would listen to those who fuel your empire.
And not just listen to counteract.

I'm sure that's not quite how it's meant to work.

Dear all Cotton Wool Spinsters,

I dare you to keep feeding your hamsters shit with sugar on.
Keep them all fuelled up enough, and they're fit to be objectified,
running on that wheel of theirs, so children will come up to the
glass and say, look, mummy, I want that one, isn't it just amazing?

Until it's all settled in.

And everything's not so amazing anymore.

MISCELLANEOUS ENTRIES OF EMMETT DOWRY

(MISCELLANEOUS ENTRY)

I am grateful that I have ended up here.

I have witnessed the deepest, darkest nights, and the brightest, most blissful days. All in the company of my cottage, full of nooks and character.

There were days I would wander into the woods, following the stream. I would research and pick mushrooms to cook with my tea that night. I would collect logs for my fire in the living room, and pick ivy, peculiar looking pebbles, funnily shaped chunks of tree bark, that I would use to weave around and fill spaces on the walls. Rabbits would stop and stare at me for a moment, before bouncing along on their merry way that day. The leaves would sway in my direction, like they were watching my back as I waded through the wood. In my later years, I would sometimes stagger and hobble with my walking stick, but I'd always find away to bid the trees a good day. I look after nature, and nature looks after me. It is a beautiful thing.

(MISCELLANEOUS ENTRY)

For the love of espresso!

The constant of my every morning.

The sun warming my face,
the breeze caressing my cheeks,

autumn leaves tapping me on the shoulder,
drops of rain washing away the dirt of my old life,
and espresso on the porch.

Feel it every day,
as one day, you will feel
for the last time.

(MISCELLANEOUS ENTRY)

If these diaries are found,
please put them into print.

I wish for the world to know,
how Infernos can shatter lives.

There must be no page numbers,
as time and place is not necessary.

Timelessness is peace.

I wish for peace.

(MISCELLANEOUS ENTRY)

Today, my hands started shaking,
and they have yet to stop.

I am struggling to write.

(MISCELLANEOUS ENTRY)

I am on the verge of
knocking on Death's door.

I am trembling
with the anticipation of it.

I will ask for Death.

Death will be with you in just a moment, Sir,
the servant will say to me.

(MISCELLANEOUS ENTRY)

Soon I will
be
running
free.

Soon I will
feel
glee.

Soon,
a great light
will wrap around me.

Gently,
softly,
kindly,

a great light
will wrap around me.

Soon I will
be a free
man
once
more.

(MISCELLANEOUS ENTRY)

A conversation with a tree.

Thank you for all you give to the world.
Thank you for living in this world, replies the tree.
Not enough people thank you, do they?
I guess not, no. That's okay. Some people aren't very thankful
though, they want to be rid of me.
Sometimes, even the most wonderful souls are abused and
overlooked.
Do you think I have a *soul?*
Of course you have a soul.

WARHOL & A FRIEND: ARTSY SEX

A knock.

Mrs, is that you darling? he says in the direction of the door.

Friend lets himself in and says: Very fucking funny Mrs Warhol.

Anyways, Andy says. On a serious note, let me show you this, I
need your opinion.

When Warhol turned around,

Friend was already lighting a spliff,

so, sharply he says: *Come!*

He throws the box of matches back onto the glass side-table

and follows Warhol to the opposite corner of the studio.

Yes, yes, go for god's sake!

he hears Warhol say,

as he

(in a friendly manner?)

shoos out a half-naked man.

Funnily enough,

Friend is not in the slightest startled, and simply, he remarks:

Another one?

Warhol tittered.

Uh—one of a few today, he's just a straggler, there's always one.

Friend eyes him up.

Your 'erotic films' are causing quite a stir, you know?

Warhol ignores him for a second, before looking up and saying:

Ah! I forgot, I'm supposed to *care,* aren't I?

Of course I know, subjectivity and all that.

Art grinds gears, it's all part of the fun.

He laughs.

Says the person who publicly said that most exciting thing about
sex

was 'not doing it'.

Yes, exactly, the most exciting thing about it is making it into an artform!
It's '63, about time this country saw some queer shit on their screens.
He pauses for a second,
and then casually says:
That guy you saw,
he was helping me shoot *Blowjob.*
Just a little project.

EIGHTH IN DRAG

I

Henry had six husbands,
all alive because even as he tried to move on,
the previous wouldn't budge.

II

Henry has the most decadent parties.

The halls were fit for celebration,
all sparkles and rainbows—
as he did quite enjoy living up to the
(somewhat damaging)
stereotype!

If one ignores the incredibly
blatant impossibility of this
(or not),
it is a story that proves to be quite entertaining.

And that is of course, that
Henry VIII is a
drag queen.

Simply imagine the aesthetic!

Tudor attire,
but vibrant and pearly,
and Henry would have their

huge wig, and dramatic eyeliner,
faux breasts and the
most extravagant heels.

They would (for lack of a better word)
slutdrop to some kind of
shit Tudor music—
which works perfectly well with the absurdity
of this entire situation;
in the centre of a cabaret layout,
surrounded by the six wives—*sorry* husbands!

III

Here's to the time's short life expectancy,
party it away.

It's chaos and beauty,
utter bent pandemonium,
and a family that lives and dies together
and big hips,
red lips,
sexy, cool,
no one's a fool—
you are all
a big Mexican wave,
passing colour from one
to the other,
above her,
the sky is a stunner.

IV

The whole occasion seems wonderful.
And it probably was.

Queer communities
didn't materialise recently.

Sorry to disappoint,
they're not a starting-out indie band,
so y'can't say
I've been there from the start,
unless you are immortal, of course.

Who are you if you
are always ruled
over by other people?

We Lay, I Fear.

Hold on,
you said,
as we make
our way to
the bed.

You are suddenly
a stranger
to
me.

Anxiety struck,
and now there is a
stranger in
my room.

I think:
Fuck,
not me, but, off!

You were my lover
and now your presence
sets
me on
ed
g
e

You smile,
Playful.
          what's wrong?
Then you're on me,
not on
on me,
just comforting.

It's scary.
unknown.
oblivion.

Maybe it's just a phase.

The Pit
of your stomach.
of emotion
of confusion
& overwhelm.

The Pit is
in your head
In your heart.

It can be
beautiful or,
sorrowful.
These can combine.
If they do so,
I'm sorry...

You may get
lost for a
little while.

Sometimes a soul may
reach out their hand,
and help you haul
yourself out.

There is a deep
melancholy
within you,
and you must wade
your way
through it

To reach the other side...

You'll get there.

I Promise,

Friend.
x

Celestial Angels:
The Noble Chandelier is suspended
from the ceiling of the Great
Ingress.

Here stood The Traitor.
The Traitor has accepted
their fate.

Each candle,
a song, at it's claws, the nectar,
sweetest spit.
At the heart of the flame.
Intense heat of the Celestials

The Empress of the Celestials
envelops them.
Jabbed a poison needle into their
slick neck swiftly.

C.A
Emmett Downy was laying on his bed.
The large window at his dormitory
graced one lucky soul who happened
to habituate there — though one
may begin to take it for granted,
with the most picturesque views
of the Mahindah Campus. The sky
bleed orange on this occasion, wore
a wrath over the campus The City
as a whole in fact. A great wrath
that held the Convirbation captive
Something so grand, miniatured by
It so vast.

Grandeur was forever meek when
something vast was concerned.
Well — this is how it seemed to
Emmett Downy.

ACKNOWLEDGEMENTS

My closest friends, I bloody love ya.
As always, the lovely family that I have.

To the art and lyricism of my biggest inspirations, I owe a lot.

AFTERWORD

Putting this collection together in hindsight of seventeen has been a pleasure. I'm glad to revisit the story that started it all, and muster up the courage to include a few other poems of mine.

ABOUT THE AUTHOR

Oliver Lewis' work has been described as "exquisite" and "a great inspiration".

He is the author of YA books: *You're Not The Only One*, and *It Breaks You Up*. 2022 saw the publication of *Celestial Angels*, a collection of poetry and vignettes.

When not writing, he also enjoys reading, seeing live music, adding to his ever-growing collection of vinyl records, and writing some more.

You can find him @oliver_reads_

Me, us, the and moon   a little note :)

I'll look up at the sky.
The moon stays hidden
    behind the odd cloud,
            occasionally peaking
                            out
    I guess we're all like a
moon, only showing certain
            aspects of ourselves.

A little at a time,
    and when we're with the
                people we love
                        most,
    On the clearest of
nights, we are completely authentically
            ourselves

June
'24
                    you're not the only one?

Obscure, fantastical, yet grounded in it's narrative of society, *Celestial Angels* tells the tale of Emmett Dowry. A life lived and documented within diaries, poetry and prose. A life of intrigue, a life shattered by the conflicts of underworld politics. An education at Masindah Academy, a youth in the city, a death in the countryside. All pieces of Emmett Dowry's puzzle.

this book is rated moderate